Dear Parents:

Children learn to read in stages, and all children develop reading skills at different ages. **Ready Readers**™ were created to promote children's interest in reading and to increase their reading skills. **Ready Readers**™ are written on two levels to accommodate children ranging in age from three through eight. These stages are meant to be used only as a guide.

Stage 1: Preschool-Grade 1
Stage 1 books are written in very short, simple sentences with large type. They are perfect for children who are getting ready to read or are just becoming familiar with reading on their own.

Stage 2: Grades 1-3
Stage 2 books have longer sentences and are a bit more complex. They are suitable for children who are able to read but still may need help.

All the **Ready Readers**™ tell varied, easy-to-follow stories and are colorfully illustrated. Reading will be fun, and soon your child will not only be ready, but eager to read.

Walter
and the Tugboat

Written by Eugene Bradley Coco
Illustrated by Edward Heck

Modern Publishing
A Division of Unisystems, Inc.
New York, New York 10022

This is Walter the whale.

Walter lives in the deep, blue sea.

Walter likes to do many things.

He likes to splash in the waves
and spout water high in the sky.

He likes to play tag
with his friends.

But most of all,
Walter likes to watch tugboats
pull ships through the sea.

Big ships.

Little ships.

Sometimes the tugboats

pull two or three ships.

Here comes a tugboat now.

Walter waves his tail
as it passes by.

Captain Jim waves back.

"I want to be a tugboat,"
says Walter.
"I want to pull ships like you do."

"You can't be a tugboat,"
laughs Captain Jim.
"You are a whale."

One day Walter sees Captain Jim's
tugboat far out at sea.
Something is wrong.

Captain Jim's tugboat
is not tugging.

"Help! Help!"
yells Captain Jim.

Walter swims out to the tugboat
as fast as he can.

"My tugboat is not big enough to pull this ship," says Captain Jim.

Walter puts the rope in his mouth
and, with all of his might,

pulls the ship to safety.

"Thank you, Walter,"
says Captain Jim.

"I guess you can be a tugboat after all."

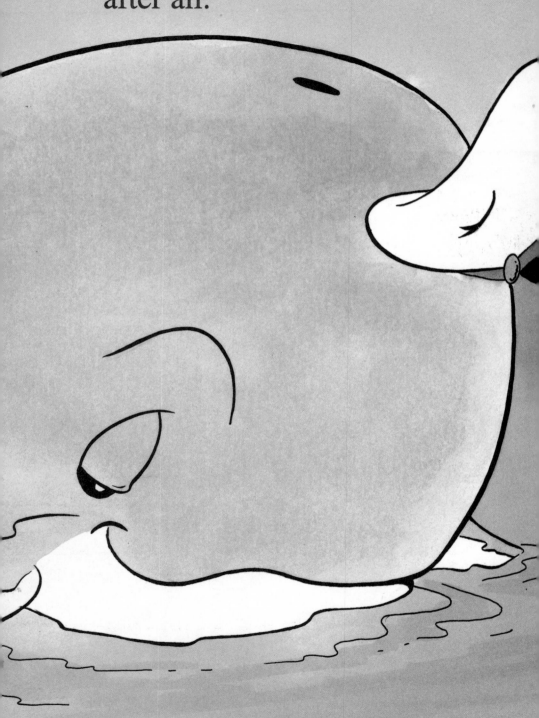

Walter smiles.
He is happy.

Now Walter is a tugboat, too.